The Magic Sneeze

Ian Whybrow

illustrated by Tony Ross

F[illegible]bb –

First published in Great Britain in 2000
by Hodder Children's Books

6 8 10 9 7 5

A Catalogue record for this book is available from the British Library.

ISBN 0340 77891 1

Printed and bound in Great Britain by
Bookmarque Ltd, Croydon, Surrey

The paper and board used in this paperback by Hodder Children's Books are natural recyclable products made from wood grown in sustainable forests. The manufacturing processes conform to the environmental regulations of the country of origin.

Hodder Children's Books
A Division of Hodder Headline Limited
338 Euston Road
London NW1 3BH

Baron Grimace

In the dark old days when Barons were brutes and castles were draughty, there was a particularly dark and dismal castle. It belonged to Baron Grimace.

Everyone feared and hated Baron Grimace. His favourite sport was "pasting the peasant". At harvest time, he would ride down the valley road to the village of Wartly and bang on the door of a poor family's cottage. "Give me three parts of your corn and vegetables!" he would cry.

If a poor father refused, because he had seven hungry mouths to feed, the Baron would shout, "Idleness! Eight people should be able to grow plenty of food! Bend over! Lazy peasants must be pasted!"

And he would boot him black and blue.

Or suppose a mother tried to explain that her seeds had not sprouted properly, so she and her family had very little to eat. The Baron would shout, "Stupidity! You should have chosen better seeds. Bend over! Stupid peasants must be pasted!"

It was just as bad for his animals.

He bit the dogs. He was horrid to his hawks. He was hard on his horses. And he never mucked out his stables. The smell was dreadful. If a visitor complained the Baron would roar, "If you think that's bad, smell this!" and he would grab them by the collar and breathe his beastly breath into their face.

There was no escape for the people he picked on. And Baron Grimace picked on everyone. Except Simmer, his cook.

In Baron Grimace's Kitchen

Baron Grimace's cook was as disgusting as his master. His name was Simmer but he was more like a boil. He was as fat and greasy as his master was huge and hairy. His fingernails were black and scratchy and he used them constantly to pick the nasty spots that covered his red, raw face.

Some said that *everything* in the kitchen went into his bubbling cooking pot if it didn't move fast enough. Woe betide the cat or the rat or the spider or the earwig that crawled across the kitchen flagstones!

The kitchen maids and the poor little slop boys were always cutting and scalding themselves. Everything they did, they did at a trot. "Quick! Or Simmer will put us in the stew! The Baron will eat us!" cried Nicholas, the servant boy.

Simmer's stews were Baron Grimace's delight. But what the Baron did not know was that it was Nicholas who made everything taste so delicious. He could not bear to touch the meat, but he was a genius with herbs and spices and vegetables. With a dash of parsley and a pinch of rosemary, he could bring out the most beautiful flavours in any dish.

Every evening, Baron Grimace set himself down at his table, banged down his fists and snuffed the air.

"Simmer!" he would cry. "I smell something scrumptious. Come, my sweet cookie. What have you got to tickle my fancy appetite? What can you serve me that is seething and succulent? What's in your stew tonight?"

Sometimes it was rabbit stew, sometimes it was wild boar stew. On very rare occasions, it was deer stew, the Baron's favourite.

Simmer would slip into the Great Hall and grin at his master. "At your ssservice, Sssire," he would hiss. "Tonight, you shall sssup on my ssspecial ssstew, Sire."

When the Baron was ready, Simmer would snap his filthy fingers and Nicholas had to ladle gallons of the stuff into the Baron's enormous bowl.

"Simmer, this is heavenly. How tender, how tasty!"

Simmer got all the praise. Poor Nicholas never got any credit for anything, no matter how succulent and special the stew was.

Nicholas was a proud boy and longed to escape from his horrible masters, but his mother, Widow Simkins, was very poor. She lived in a tiny cottage on the outskirts of Wartly village, close to the edge of the forest. The only pennies she had for herself were the few that Nicholas earned for her. How he wished that he could make her hard life happier.

Hunting the Deer

After "pasting the peasant", Baron Grimace's second favourite sport was hunting. He had a great collection of traps and nets and spears and cross-bows, and he loved chasing creatures and killing them.

"If you can't eat them, stuff them!" was his motto. So no hedgehog or badger, no vole or mole was safe when Baron Grimace was about.

Not far away, to the east of the village of Wartly, was a wonderfully wide and leafy forest. Every day the Baron rode off there to try out his traps and weapons.

Above all, he loved to hunt deer, for remember, deer stew was his great delight. For an extra pleasure, he would decorate the walls of his castle with the heads of the unlucky creatures. So, while he sucked their bones, he could amuse himself by tossing up his cap to see if he could catch it on their horns.

One morning, the Baron was crashing through the forest with Sir Roger de Posh and a crowd of riders and hounds. Suddenly he spied, far off, two deer. One was a magnificent female and the other, her wide-eyed baby.

"Double delicious!" roared the Baron. "A doe and her fawn! Tally ho!"

The deer were quick but the whipped horses and the dogs were quicker. No matter how she twisted and turned with her baby at her heels, the doe could not shake off the hunters. Terrified and tired, the deer were chased out of the shelter of the trees.

Out into the open, they raced, over the fields and into the muddy lane that led to the village.

Almost at their last gasp, the beautiful creatures reached the outskirts of Wartly. In a last effort to save themselves, they leapt over a stick fence – and into Widow Simkins' tiny garden.

Widow Simkins

Widow Simkins had been weeding in her cabbage patch when she heard dogs baying in the distance.

"Some poor creature is about to be torn to pieces!" she muttered. "I wish I could do something to help."

Just a few minutes later, the terrified deer and her baby flew over her fence and tried to shelter behind it. The savage hounds were close behind but Widow Simkins was brave. She gripped her hoe like a quarter staff and set her feet firmly apart. As the first hound came over the sticks – *whack!* – she sent him howling back over it.

Whack! Away went another!

But before long, the riders caught up and the dogs returned.

They trampled down the fence and their horses smashed the vegetables under their hooves. They found the widow, standing like a soldier with her back to the door and the deer behind her. The fierce hounds growled and snapped, ready to tear her to pieces. Her strength was almost spent, but just then came the sound of a horn and snap of the hunters' whips.

"Stand aside, Widow! You will spoil my supper!" It was the Baron's thundering voice.

"Never!" called Widow Simkins. "I know what it is to be a mother! And if you kill these pretty creatures, then you must kill me too."

The Baron was struck dumb. No one had spoken like this to him before. He thought of giving her a pasting with his boot – but hesitated. She was little, but she had spirit. She looked as if she would put up a good fight.

Behind him, Sir Roger laughed. "We've had good sport, Baron. Get a net on the mother deer and let the widow keep the fawn. She may change her mind about killing it yet. For look, we have left her no cabbages or carrots for her pot."

"A fine idea, Sir Roger!" laughed the Baron. "You men, get the net over that doe!"

It took two strong men to hold the widow. She struggled bravely but they were too much for her.

When the mother deer was caught and tied in the net, the Baron spied the widow's hens. "Take those, too!" he ordered. "And bring the cow. She shall drink no more milk neither!"

At last, the cruel Baron pulled his horse's head round and gave him a dig with his spurs. "Away, huntsmen!" he bawled. "Keep the fawn, Widow. For now. You may fatten it up for me. And tonight your boy Nicholas will be pasted for your rudeness to me, make no mistake!"

Widow Simkins sank slowly to the ground as the hunt galloped away from her ruined garden. The little fawn licked her tears.

Aunty Boots

And indeed poor Nicholas got a worse pasting than ever that night. His ear stung, his backside was black and blue. When Simmer lost his temper and started flinging pots and pans at his head, the lad could take no more. He dashed out the door and ran for his life.

Along the valley road he sped, not pausing for breath until he reached the forest. He dare not go to his mother's house, for they would look for him there first. Instead, following a narrow path he knew well, he groped his way till he came to a cottage with a twisty chimney on the far side of the forest. It was damp and dripping and shadowy. Just the place for a witch to dwell.

Nicholas tapped nervously on the door. He had to wait. And wait. He thought he heard something. Was it a lizard scuttling across dry leaves? Or an owl clicking its claws on the rafters of the dim parlour?

It was both of those. Nicholas shivered.

"Come you in!" called a shrill voice.

The door creaked like a raven as the boy pushed on it. It took a moment for his eyes to become accustomed to the gloom.

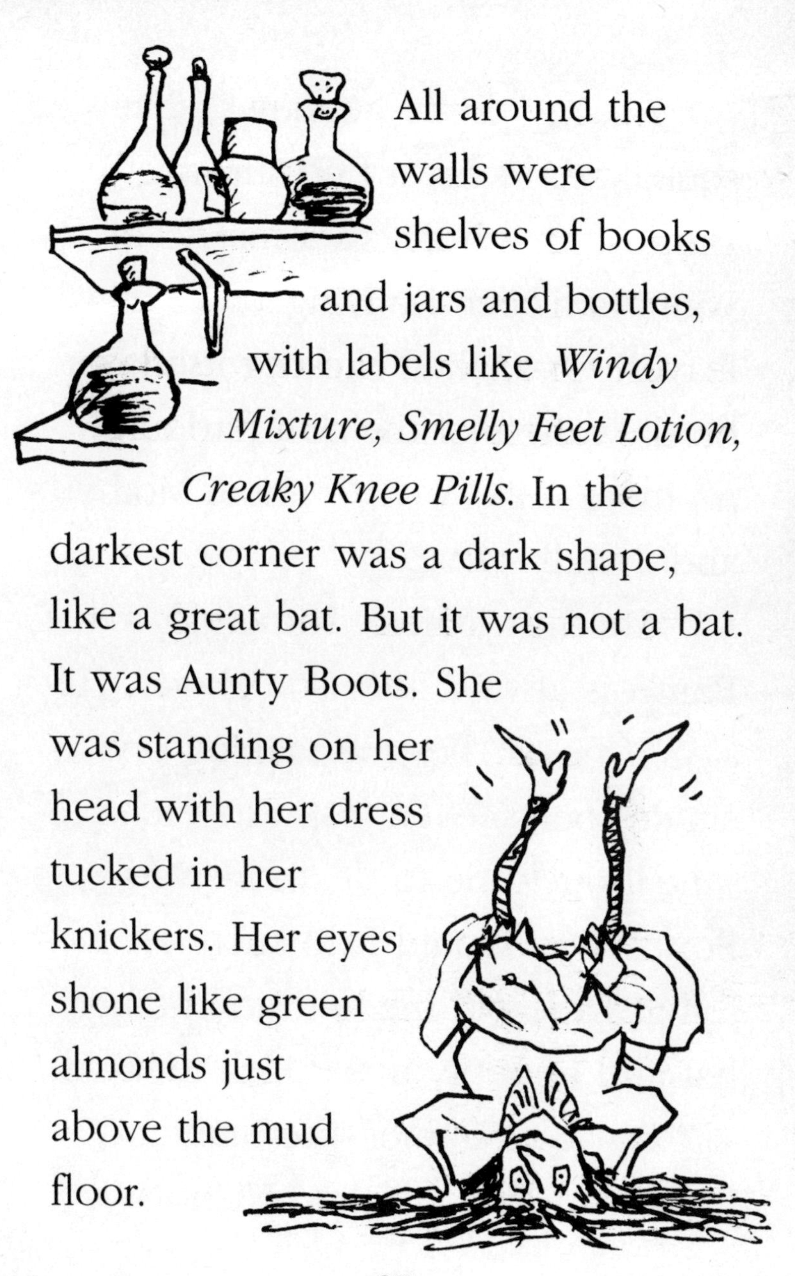

All around the walls were shelves of books and jars and bottles, with labels like *Windy Mixture, Smelly Feet Lotion, Creaky Knee Pills.* In the darkest corner was a dark shape, like a great bat. But it was not a bat. It was Aunty Boots. She was standing on her head with her dress tucked in her knickers. Her eyes shone like green almonds just above the mud floor.

"Ah, my pretty nephew!" she squeaked. "What a fine surprise! I suppose that brute of a master of yours has been bullying you again."

"They've taken our cow and our hens! We shall have no more eggs, no more milk! We're ruined! Mother and I shall starve."

"Ah, the villains!" she cried. "That Baron is always after somebody. He says if he catches me making one single spell – even just a love charm – he'll duck me to death in Wartly Pond! Now would I do such a thing? Little old me with my pointy hat and knobbly nose? Heh heh!"

"I've got Simmer after me, and Baron Grimace," sighed Nicholas.

"I dare not go home to mother. May I hide here with you?"

"Now, now, don't upset yourself. You're safe here for a while. Let Aunty see what she can do!" she squeaked. "But just give me a minute, dearie. I must get the blood to my head. I'm warming up a couple of my crafty ideas for the book I'm writing. It's called *Mistress Boots' Book of Cures.*"

"Woo-hoo! Kark!" The boy looked up. Above his head, a row of owlets and a raven with a wooden leg shifted and blinked down at him from the rafters.

"All right, my birds, be still," cooed Aunty Boots. "Nicholas, you are not to worry. Now, be a good boy; pop into the scullery and check my cauldron for me. If you hear it bubbling, damp down the fire. But mind, whatever you do, *don't* lift the lid!"

"Aunty! What are you cooking?" Nicholas lowered his voice to a whisper. "Is it something magic?"

"Ask me no questions and I'll tell you no lies," cackled Aunty Boots. "And *don't* lift the lid."

Lifting the Lid

What boy with any spirit or curiosity could stop himself lifting that lid? Not Nicholas.

He stood for a moment with his ear close to the sooty side of the great, round pot. He was used to listening for stews to come to the boil but the sound he heard now was new.

There was a sort of a humming. A sort of a singing. Or was it like waves, perhaps? It was too tempting. In a trice, the lid was off.

At once, a delicious smell rose from the mixture. "What can it be?" thought Nicholas. He moved his nose a little closer. A *little* closer. He sniffed deeply.

Nicholas was thrown against the wall by a howling wind. It whirled about the little house like a tornado.

Plates and dusty books flew like birds, and birds crashed to the floor like plates, until with a screech and a roar like a furious dragon, the wind gathered itself into a narrow, twisting coil and vanished up the chimney.

The First Sneeze

When Nicholas came to (for he had fainted clean away) it was morning. He was puzzled to see a jewel of some kind hanging over him.

It twinkled and sparkled in a thin beam of sunlight. As his eyes became clearer, he realized it was not a jewel, but a little drop of moisture that dangled from the knobbly nose of his Aunty Boots.

"Oo, you are an inquisitive chappy, aren't you! I ought to have guessed you'd never be able to keep your nose out of my business." Then, gently, she mopped his forehead with a cool wet cloth, and asked him how he was feeling.

"Wh . . . what habbened?" said Nicholas. His nose felt sore. Had he fallen on it?

"To tell you the truth, I'm not quite certain," said Aunty Boots. "I was working on a cure for the flu. It's a new mixture, a strong one – that's why I wanted the lid left on! I hope I haven't made a mistake."

Aunty Boots started flicking through the pages of a thick book with stars and half moons on the cover. She was muttering to herself.

"Not a dragon . . . hmmm . . . Too much knotweed, perhaps. Did I overdo it with the snails' trails? Possibly. What did I put in after that pinch of dried toad sweat? The six moth tongues? Yes . . . or was it seven?" She turned to her nephew again. "Now, think! Nicholas, can you remember anything? Did you see anything mighty when you lifted the lid? Anything powerful? Any giants? Any ogres?"

"No."

"Any dinosaurs?"

"No. Id was invisible."

Aunty Boots gasped. "Invisible, you say! A mighty *invisible* force . . . oh no. It couldn't be, surely . . .!"

Nicholas could feel a sneeze coming. Ahhh . . .

"Nicholas!" shouted Aunty Boots. "Pay attention now. This mighty force. You didn't happen to sniff it did you? Nicholas . . ."

Nicholas's nose was itching. It was bursting. "Ahhh . . . ahhh . . ."

Aunty Boots shook him. "Nicholas! Look at me. Speak to me! DID YOU SNIFF THAT SPELL? Nicholas . . ."

"AHHH – WISHOOOO!"

A Wasp

No sooner had Nicholas sneezed than something strange began to happen to his aunt.

Her knobbly nose folded in to a black blob and her eyes shifted to the top of her head. Her body turned bright yellow with black hoops round it.

Her waist squeezed in. Her arms became transparent wings, she grew three pairs of long hairy legs, and a nasty, pointed sting.

She rose into the air with a loud buzz. She flitted once round the room, banging into things – and then shot out of the window, into the garden.

"Aunty! Don't leave me! Cub bag!" wailed Nicholas. He grabbed a butterfly net and dashed out of the door after her.

At the far end of the untidy garden, past the healing herbs and the plants she grew for magic, there grew a scratchy, catchy bramble bush. High up among the thorny branches was a cluster of fat blackberries, bursting with juice. The wasp buzzed greedily towards the juiciest berry of the bunch. Nicholas reached forward with the net. Closer. Closer. But just as the wasp was settling . . .

CRASH!

. . . it turned back into Aunty Boots who fell with a scream into the middle of the prickly bush.

"Nicholas!" she yelled, struggling to untangle herself. "Think quickly! What was in your mind before you sneezed?"

"Sorry, Aunty. You were getting on my nerves a bit." He poked about with the butterfly net to try to free her.

"Yes, yes, I understand that. But what were you thinking?"

"Well . . . I just wished you would buzz off."

"Did you say you wished?" she gasped. "You wished I'd buzz off and off I buzzed! Do you know what this means?"

"No," said Nicholas.

"It means that you have a mighty powerful spell up your nose! I was trying to cook up a cure for the flu, but somehow I've created a spell with a great deal of mischief in it! Now you just be careful. Whatever you do, do not wish anything. It could be dangerous. And *above all* try not to sneeze."

Trying Not to Wish

How could Nicholas *stop* wishing? The poor boy had no job and no money. He wanted to look after his mother, but he couldn't stay at her cottage without the Baron's men knowing where to find him. His mother had not even a drop of milk or a hen's egg to keep her from starving, only a few squashed vegetables.

"Can't I just wish for an army to help me fight the Baron?" said Nicholas.

"The spell might get you an army, but how long will the wish last? A magic army might not do what you command. It might disappear in the middle of the fight. It might fight the wrong people," said Aunty Boots. "Remember, there's mischief up your nose. Keep it there; that's my advice. Don't do any wishing at all. It's too dangerous."

"Well, can't *you* do something to help mother, Aunty?"

"I haven't got any magic that will help her at the moment, I'm not that sort of witch," said Aunty Boots.

"Cures are my thing. So it would be better if I stayed here and tried to find one for your little problem. But we mustn't let your mother worry on her own. You must disguise yourself and go and tell her that you're safe. Smuggle her in a bit of breakfast, while you're at it."

So Aunty Boots sorted Nicholas out a nice disguise (a ginger wig, an orange frock and a scarf to cover his face), and sent him with a basket of goodies to the village of Wartly.

It was a good idea. Nice and simple. Nothing could go wrong. Except that the forest was full of the Baron's men.

So before the church bell sounded midday, Aunty Boots had been captured and dumped in the darkest dungeon of Grimace Castle. As for Nicholas, he was being dragged kicking and screaming back down the stone stairs to Simmer's kitchen.

Back in the Kitchen

"Ssso," hissed Simmer. "You thought you could run away from your duties. Do you sssee this thick ear? The Baron gave me that. He said I ssserved him *muck* for his ssssupper last night. He said I was sloppy. He said *I* was losing my touch.

"Now the Baron wants a special stew tonight, with all the trimmings.

So get on with it! And if I don't get back in his good books – I'll show *you* who's lost his touch! I'll show *you* a touch or two with my ladle!"

So Nicholas set to, peeling and weighing the potatoes and carrots, measuring and sprinkling the herbs and spices. As he worked, he looked round the smoky, steamy kitchen walls and his eyes fell on a terribly sad sight.

"Blast these onions!" sniffed Nicholas, as a tear dropped on to the table.

Pass the Pepper

The stew that Nicholas served that night was the most delicious that the Baron had ever tasted. He made Simmer and Nicholas stand by while he gobbled it up.

"Just what I need to build up my strength, Simmer!" he shouted, smacking his lips. "I shall need it for ducking that witch in Wartly Pond tomorrow morning!

"Hmm, lovely stew. Wonderful!

Almost perfect. It just needs a dash *more* of something. What do you say, Nicholas? A couple of slugs? A pinch of dried cowpat?"

"I don't know, Sire," said Nicholas, waiting for his smack round the head.

"Spoilsport!" roared the Baron. "Do you think it lacks anything, Simmer?"

"Whatever my wise lord wishes," crawled Simmer. "Sssome ssslug ssspit, perhapsss? Sssome monkey brain? Yesss? SSS SSS SSS!"

Nicholas looked up and saw the heads of all the hunted animals looking sadly down from the walls of the Great Hall.

"I wish . . ." he thought. Then he stopped himself. Too dangerous. Remember what Aunty Boots said.

"Speak up, boy! Let's have a laugh, boy."

"It might be dangerous, Sire," said Nicholas.

"Risk it, boy, risk it!" shouted the Baron.

"Then try a little pepper, Sire."

"A *little* pepper!" said the Baron. "I've never had a *little* of anything I've liked in my life. There!" With that, he took the pepper pot and shook a mighty cloud of the stuff on Nicholas's head. "HA HA! GOTCHA!" he laughed.

"Ah . . . ahhh . . ." said Nicholas.

"AHHH . . . WISHOO!"

Revenge of the Animals

From the walls came a bellowing, a growling, a snorting. It was the angry cries of a great host of forest creatures! Out of the stewpot rose other sounds: a loud mooing, a loud clucking, and the rasping call of a deer.

And suddenly the Great Hall of Grimace Castle was alive with animals. Tame beasts and wild beasts together barged the Baron off his seat and chased the cook round the table. They pecked and butted and bit and bucked, but most of all, they *booted* the Baron and his crook of a cook. They *booted* their bottoms black and blue.

"Help! Somebody save us!" wailed Simmer, but a deer, a buck with magnificent horns, lowered his head. By his side, proud and angry, stood the doe that popped out of the stewpot. The doe nodded and the buck heaved the cook high into the air – and out of the window.

Away he flew into the moat, where he sank like a stone.

"Mercy!" groaned Baron Grimace. "Keep that cow away from me! Get these chickens off me! Save me from this mad mountain goat!"

Nicholas raised his arms and all the animals stood still. He held out his hand. "The key to the dungeon! Now!" he ordered.

A few minutes later, Aunty Boots was in the Great Hall and dancing with delight to see that the Baron had found out for himself what it was like to be pasted.

But all of a sudden, the animals let the Baron alone. They ran to the open windows. The wild ones snuffed the fresh and leafy smell of the forest. Daisy and the hens caught sight of their dear old cottage in the village, and the doe's ears pricked up as she heard her baby calling her. With a great cry of joy, they galloped as one out of the Hall. They kicked down every door until they came to the main gate.

Then they clattered over the drawbridge to freedom.

"You two will pay with your lives for this!" roared the Baron. "Guards! Clap these two in irons!"

Heavy boots sounded on the stairs. The castle guards with magnificent eagle feathers nodding on their helmets rushed into the room. As the Captain of the Guard himself bent to lock the chains on Nicholas's wrists, the tip of an eagle feather tickled Nicholas's nose.

Aunty whispered a warning. "Be careful, Nicholas! Wishes usually come in threes. You used one of yours by turning me into a wasp and another by bringing the animals back to life. Wish for something that will bring a happy ending!"

"Ah . . . ahhh . . ." said Nicholas as the feather bobbed under his nose. What could he wish for that would make everything right? Quick! Think!

"Serves you right if the handcuffs hurt!" said the Baron.

"AHHHH-WISHOOO!" said Nicholas.

And that was wish number three.

Third Time Lucky

Whoever would have thought that wicked Baron Grimace was the marrying kind?

I mean, wasn't it odd that Baron Grimace should fall in love with Widow Simkins and beg her to marry him?

Wasn't it strange that the Baron was rather handsome (after a bath and a haircut)? All the villagers thought so. They also thought it was amazing that their nasty old Baron had suddenly turned into the kindest, most generous master any peasant could hope for.

The wedding feast was quite wonderful. It was completely vegetarian, and it was prepared by the youngest, richest and most famous chef in the world, Nicholas Simkins.

There were fireworks down by the pond to celebrate the great day. Aunty Boots lit the bonfire. She had made it herself out of the wood from a chopped-up ducking stool.

She was the happiest guest at the wedding. Thanks to a generous grant from the Baron, she had bought a little shop and sold cures.

People came from all over the kingdom to buy them.

"The Baron's so much nicer than he used to be. It's like a wish come true," she used to say to Nicholas with a laugh and a wink.

And Nicholas would smile back and tap his marvellous nose.